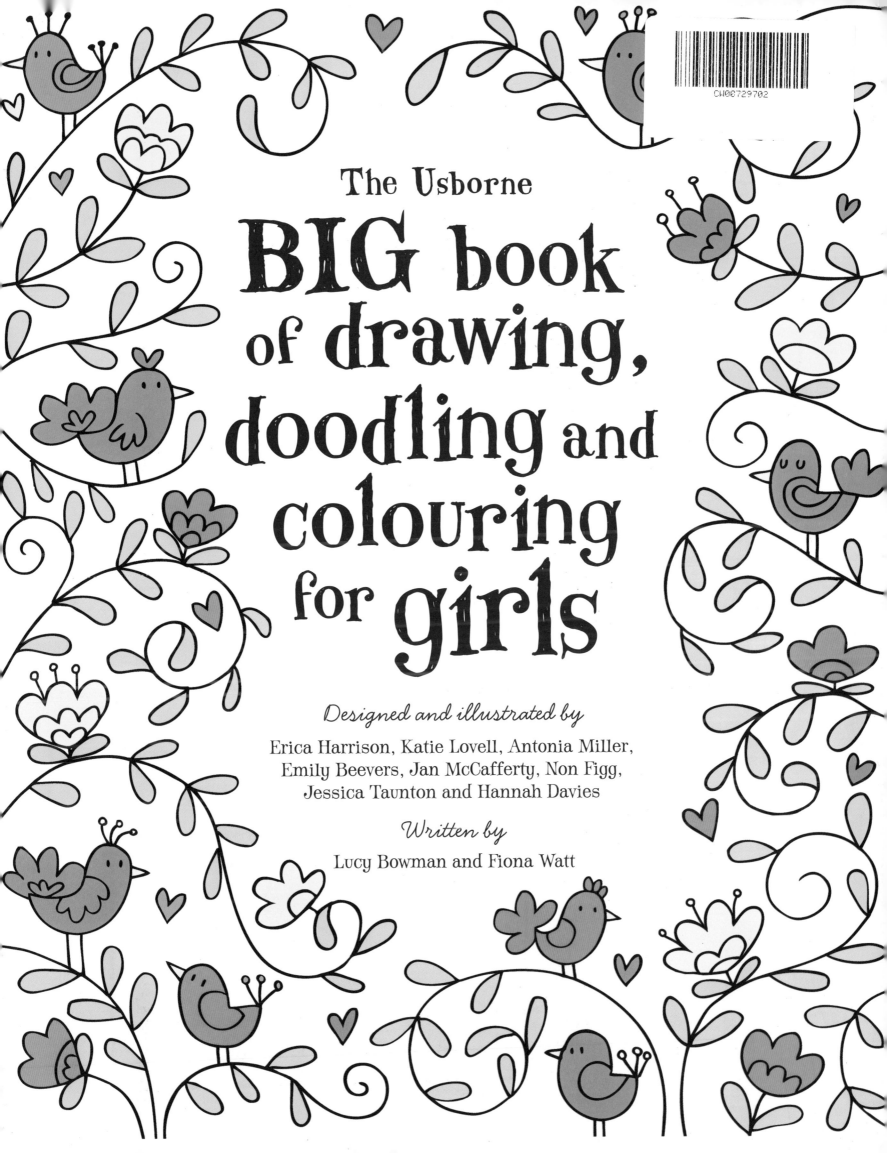

The Usborne
BIG book
of drawing,
doodling and
colouring
for girls

Designed and illustrated by

Erica Harrison, Katie Lovell, Antonia Miller,
Emily Beevers, Jan McCafferty, Non Figg,
Jessica Taunton and Hannah Davies

Written by

Lucy Bowman and Fiona Watt

How to use this book...

On some of the pages you'll find ideas for what to do, but you can do whatever you like.

Use pens, pencils or crayons to complete the pictures.

You could fill in large areas, or add stripes, spots or patterns of your own.

When you draw on top of a shape with a pen, wait for a couple of seconds for the ink to dry, so that it doesn't smudge.

Fill in some of the shapes.

Doodle more fluttering butterflies.

Draw different faces on these animal heads.

How many greens and yellows do you have? Use them to fill in the forest.

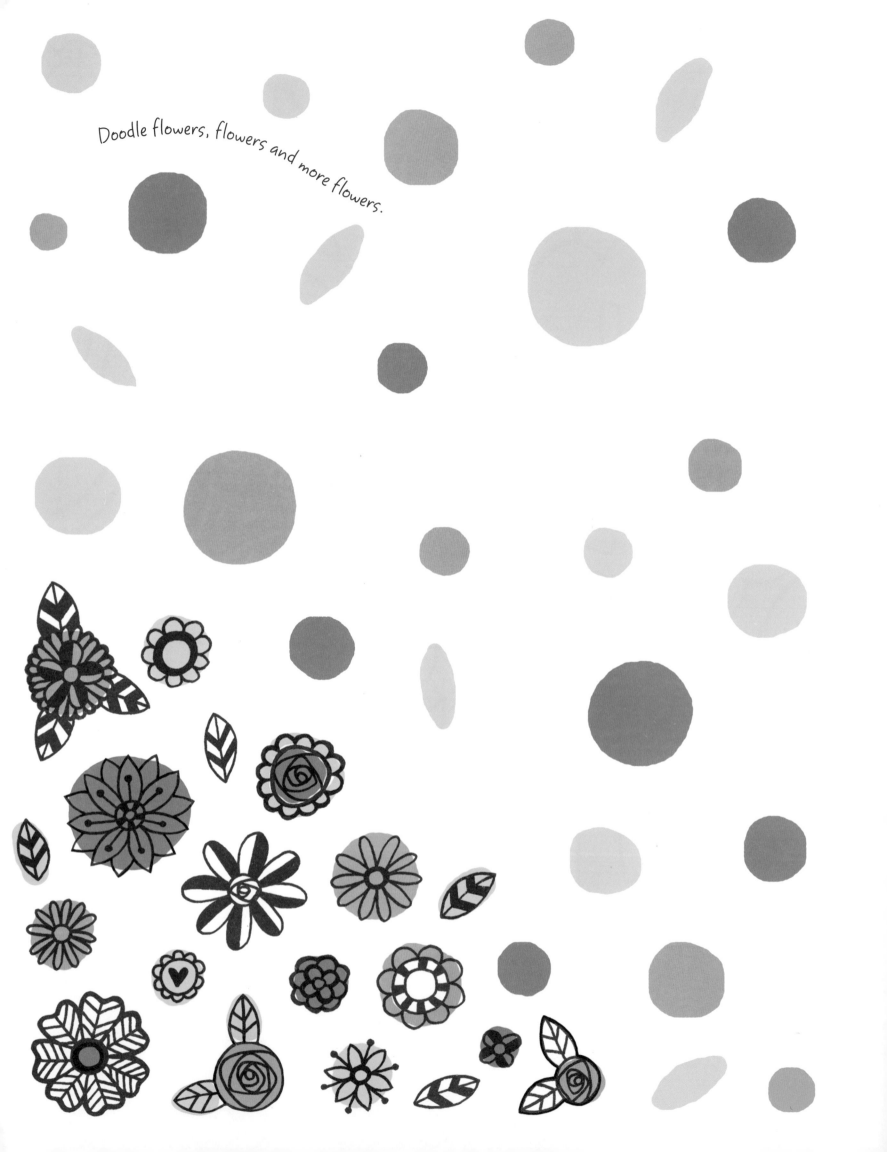

Doodle flowers, flowers and more flowers.

Finish these rows of houses.

Add doors, windows and decorations. Who do you think lives inside?

How many different outfits can you design?

Monsters marching across the pages...

Doodle clouds, stars, planets and birds.

Draw lots of flowers.

Add some busy bugs, too.

Buzzzzz

Add lots of patterns to the buildings and roofs.

It's a sunny day, so fill the washing line with clothes.

Odd socks...

Make them pairs.

Turn these shapes into faces.

R ahil

millie

Ollie

Luca

brandon

Gefin

Sam

Freddie

by Luca Name: Evil bean

bobby alien

BOB

Maybe give some of them names?

taylor (terd)

Grary (Garry)

Ivan

Ali

Reko (Rump)

Laddy oraga

Draw more flowers then add stalks and leaves.

Fill this side with hearts...

...and this side with stars.

Doodle patterns on these fantastic flamingoes.

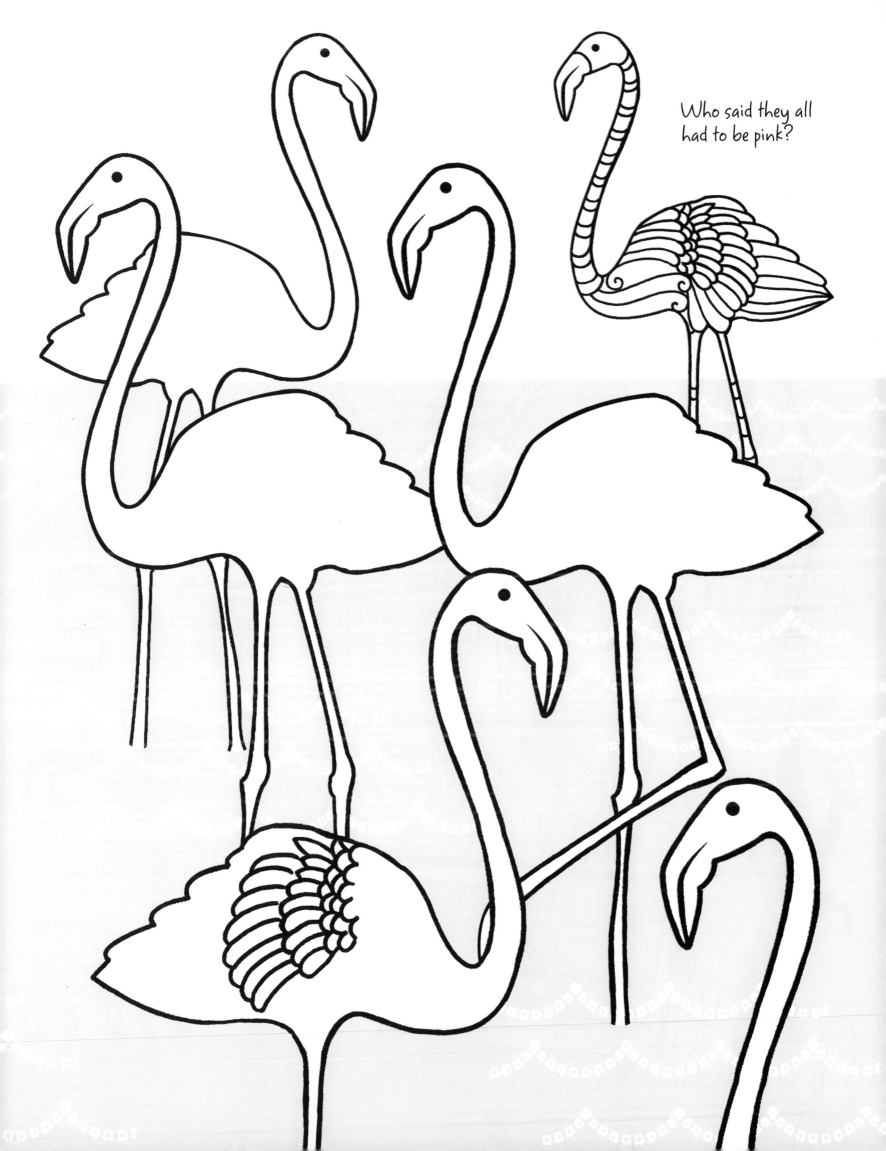

Who said they all had to be pink?

Draw scary things in the windows and more bats fluttering around.

Finish the tiaras, then doodle more.

Design the buildings, then fill the streets with shoppers.

Some of these shells need a snail...

...and some of these snails need a shell.

Fill in the ice-cream cones and doodle on yummy toppings.

FLASH

Make the audience even bigger.

Who is holding this camera?

Join the shapes with doodled patterns.

Doodle more rainbows, clouds and stars all over these pages.

Where are the rest of the dogs?

Give them bones to chew and toys to play with.

Draw more swimming mermaids...

...and bubbles floating in the water.

Doodle windows and draw more trees, buildings and clouds.

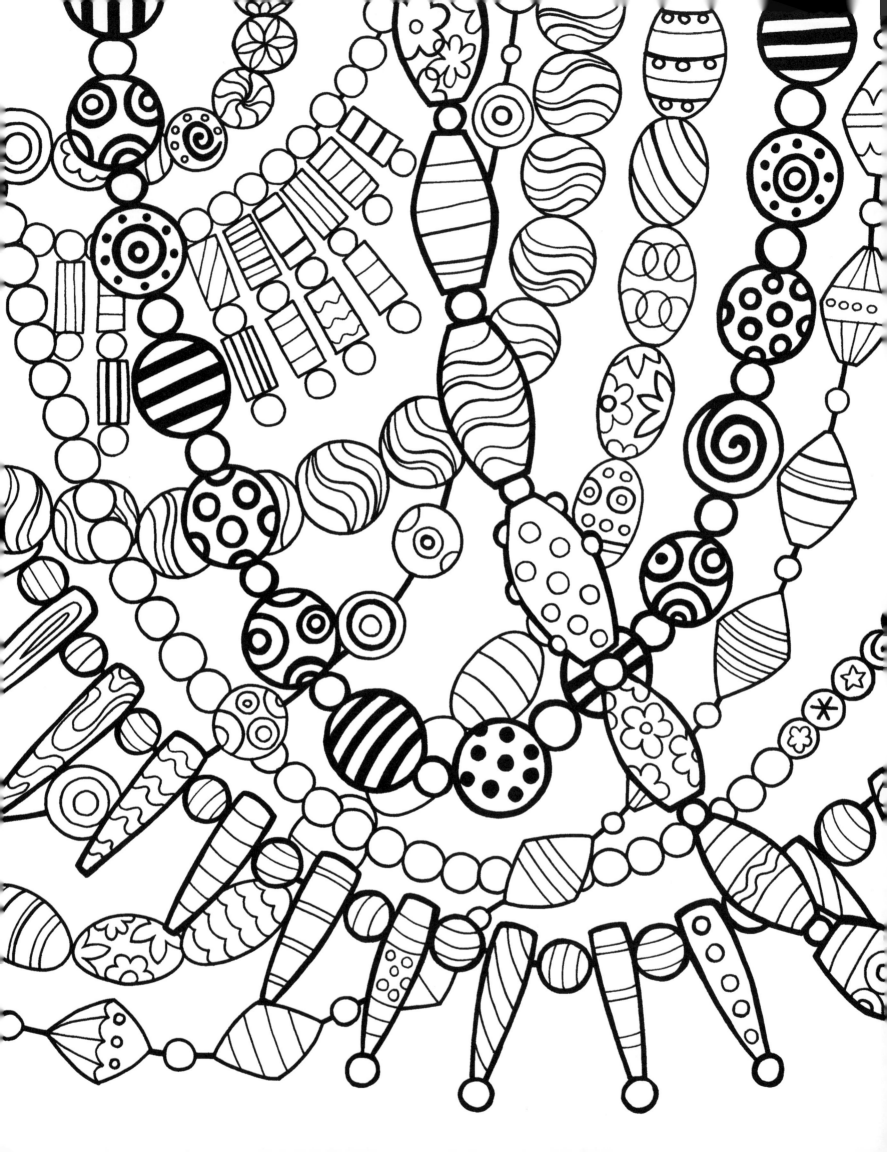

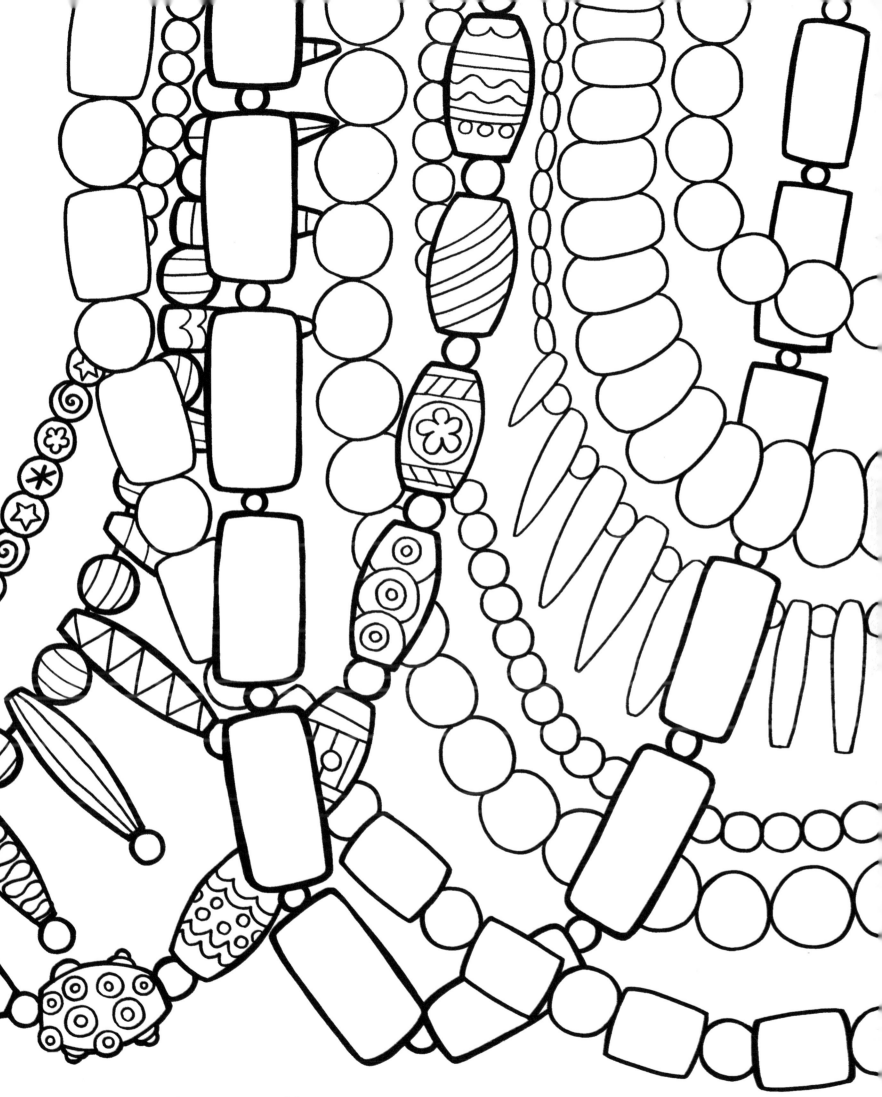

Fill in as many beads as you like.

Doodle more branches.

Doodle more birds.

Doodle more flowers.

Doodle patterns on the shells.

Fill this page with shoes...

...and this page with bags.

These tea things need decorating...

Doodle amazing wigs on the actresses and actor.

Fill the pages with patterned bugs.

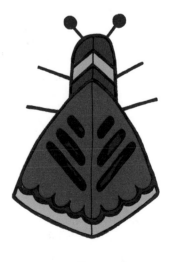

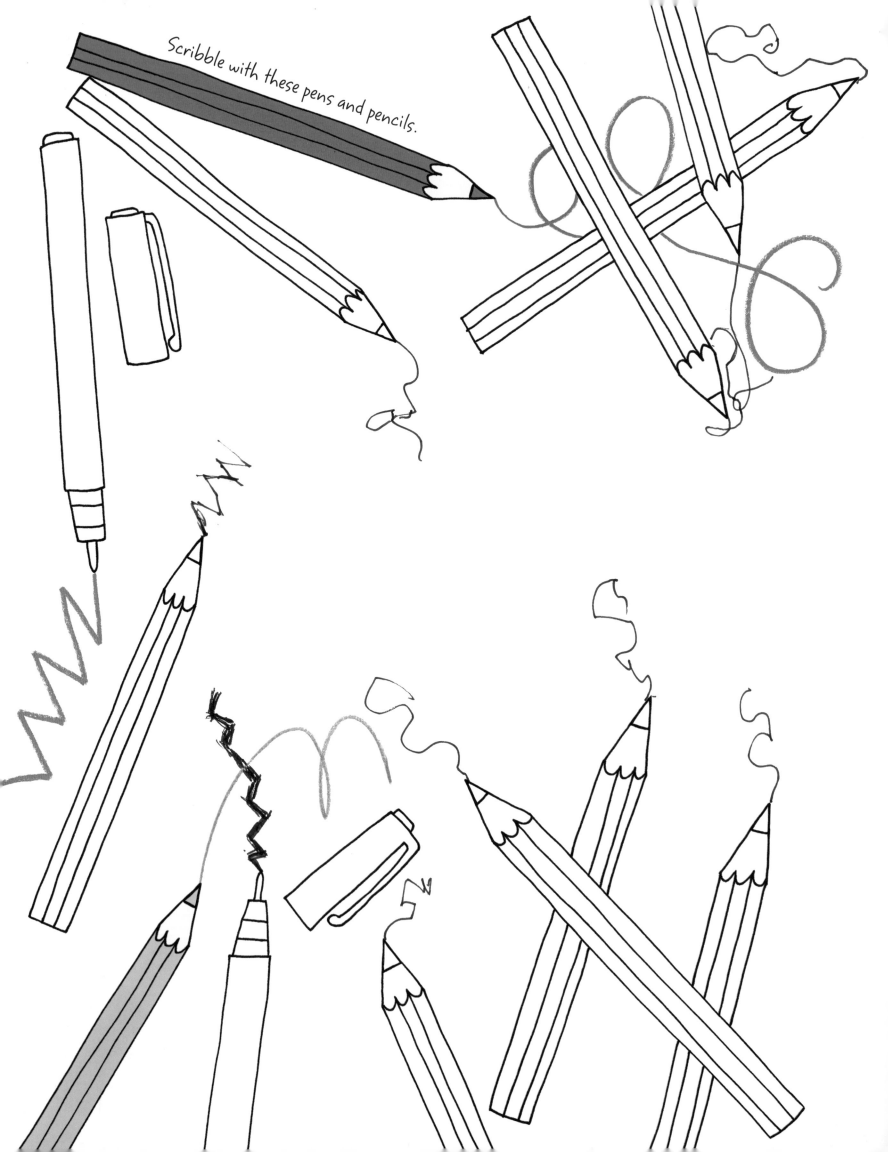

Scribble with these pens and pencils.

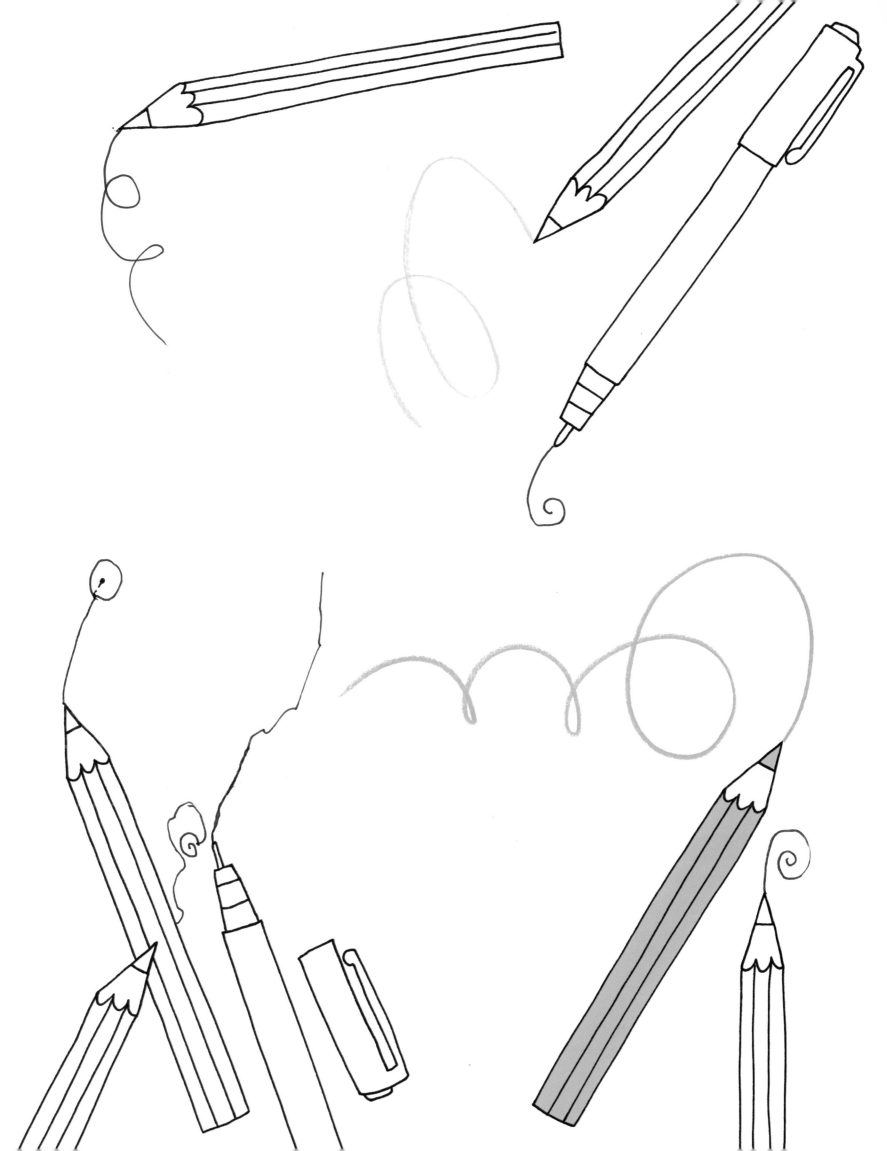

Design some dresses and accessories.

Some bats are flying; others are hanging in the trees.

Draw faces and patterns on these owls.

Fill the pages with supergirls.

Whoosh!

Fill the gaps with swirly patterns.

Decorate these nails.

Which shades will you choose?

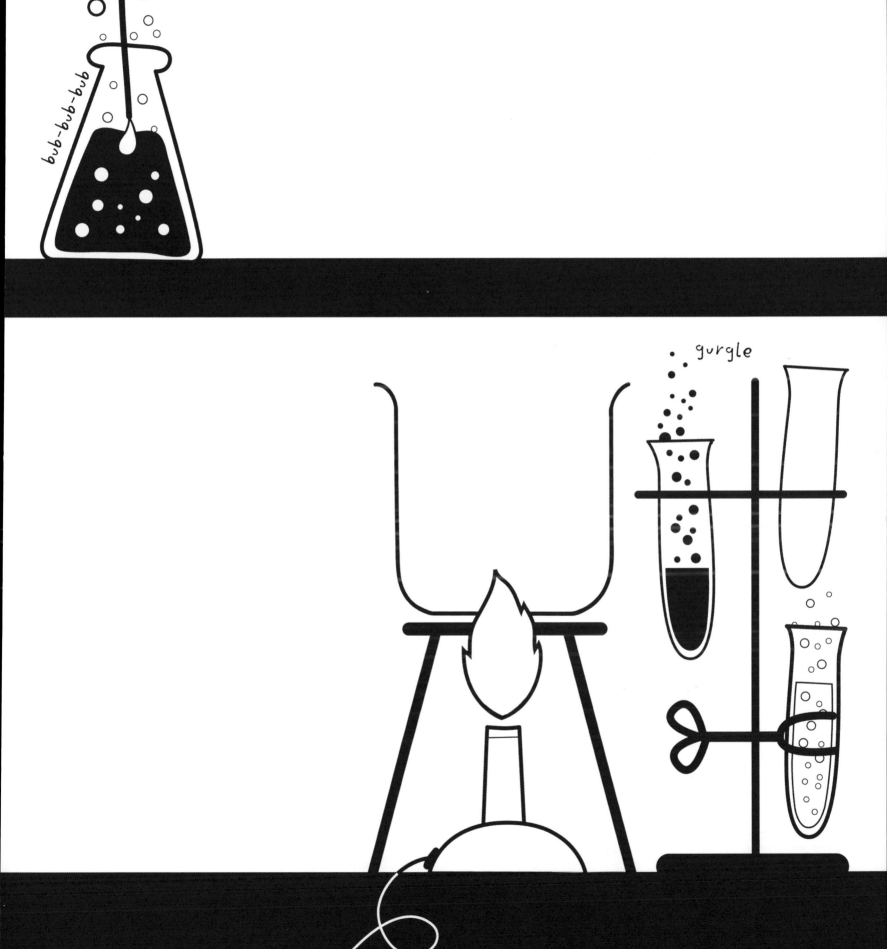

Draw more partying penguins.

Fill the pages with hundreds of circles.

Create a collection of
exquisite perfume bottles.

Sketch more jumping horses.

Straight...curly...
long...short?
Create different
hairstyles.

Add earrings, bows, glasses and other accessories, too.

Continue this red and black doodle.

Turn these shapes into monsters.

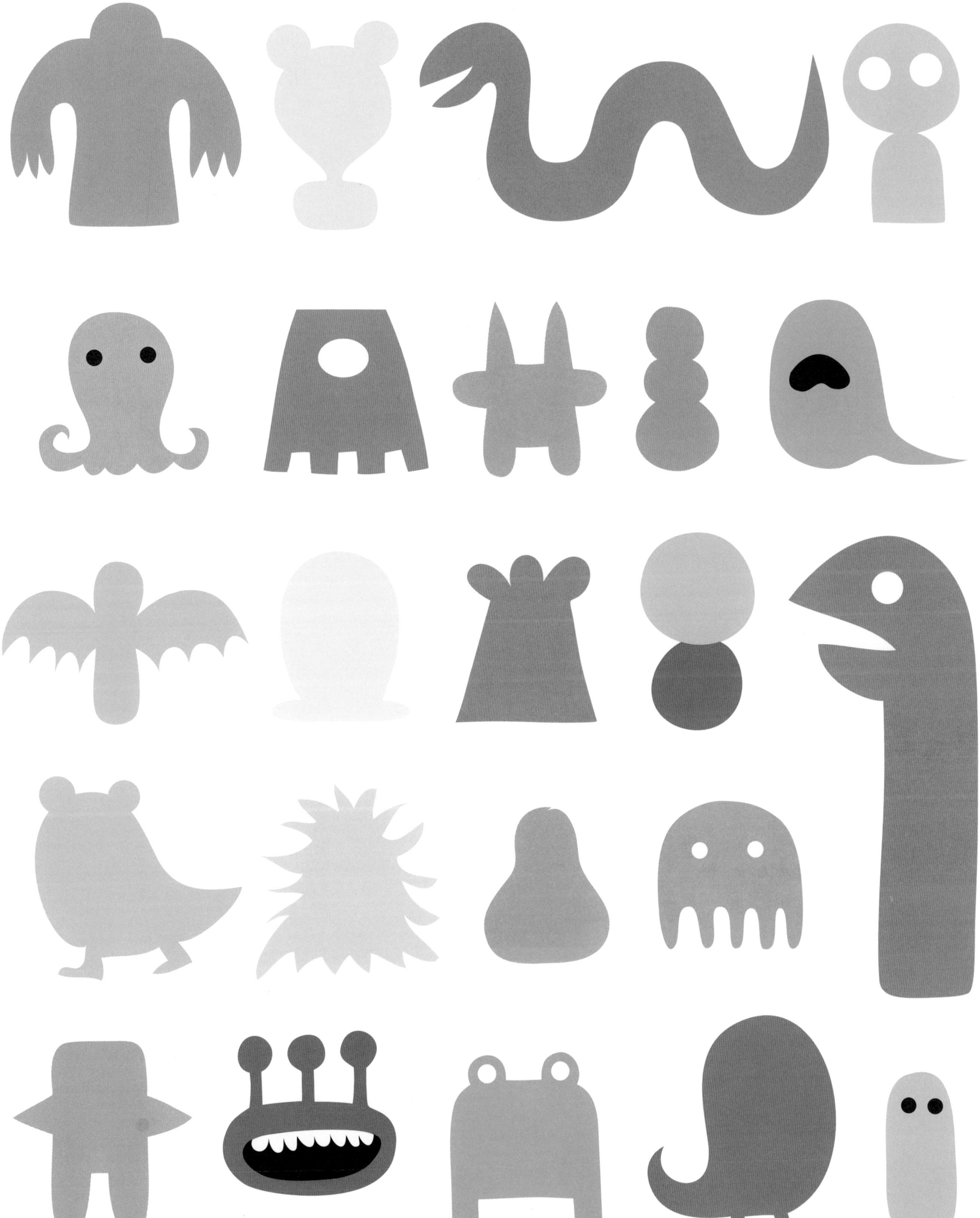

Fill in these dancers' dresses with delicate patterns.

Doodle decorations
in their hair.

Fill the pages
with patterns.

Doodle on the stamps and envelopes.

Doodle more caterpillars and tasty leaves.

Munch, munch, munch...

Draw more traffic on the busy roads.

Fill the shelves with pretty perfume bottles...
or anything else you like.

Doodle patterns on
the flowers.

Doodle lots and lots of buttons until there is room for no more.

Draw more rabbits...

...flowers...

...and crunchy carrots.

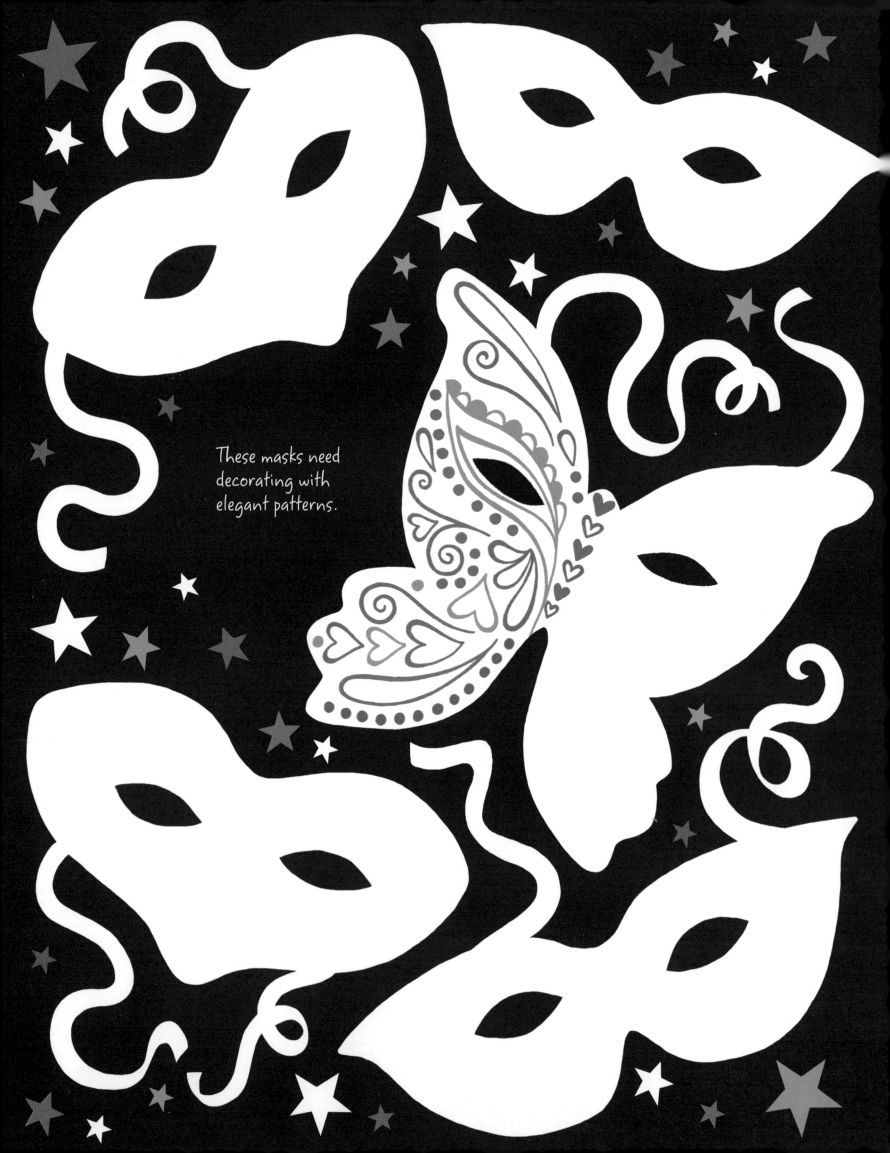

These masks need decorating with elegant patterns.

Roses, roses everywhere...fill the pages with more.

Decorate the Russian matryoshka dolls.

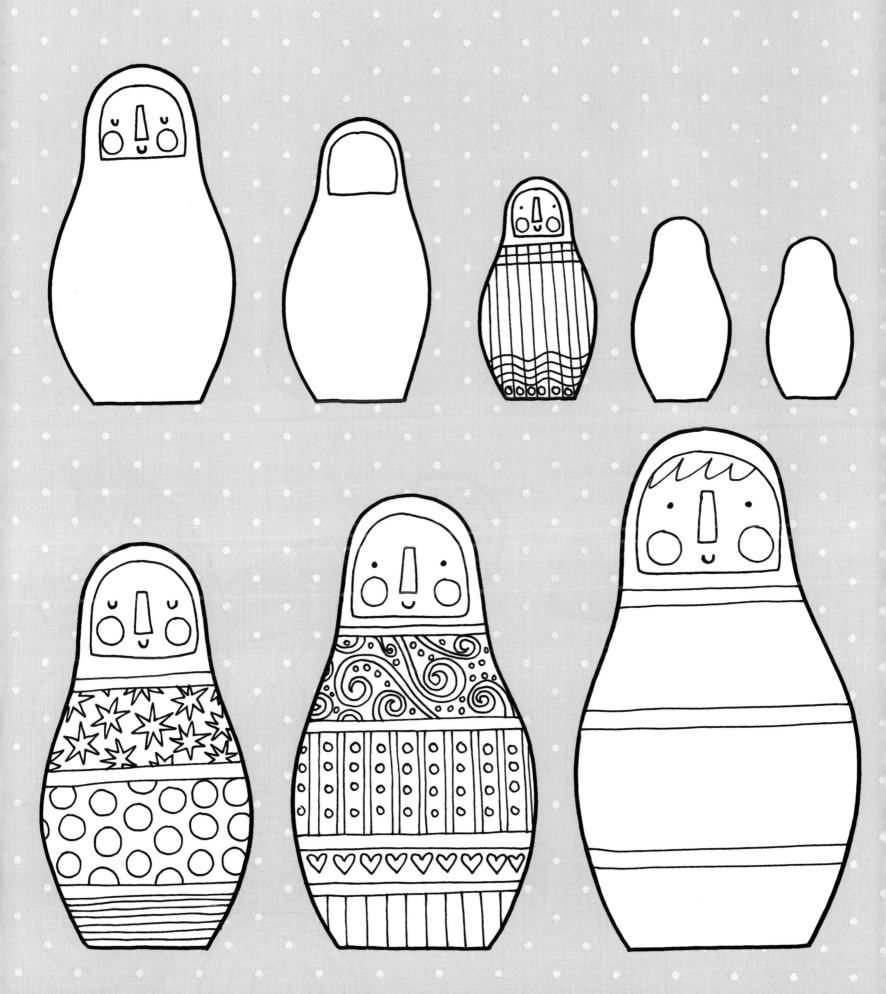

Doodle more bright shapes.

Give us stripes or spots, bells or bows...

Decorate these hearts.

These sweet treats have just
been baked and decorated.

Cover the pages
with more cupcakes
and cookies.

Doodle patterns
on these flamenco
dancers' dresses.

Add frills
and flowers
to their hair.

Build the robots.

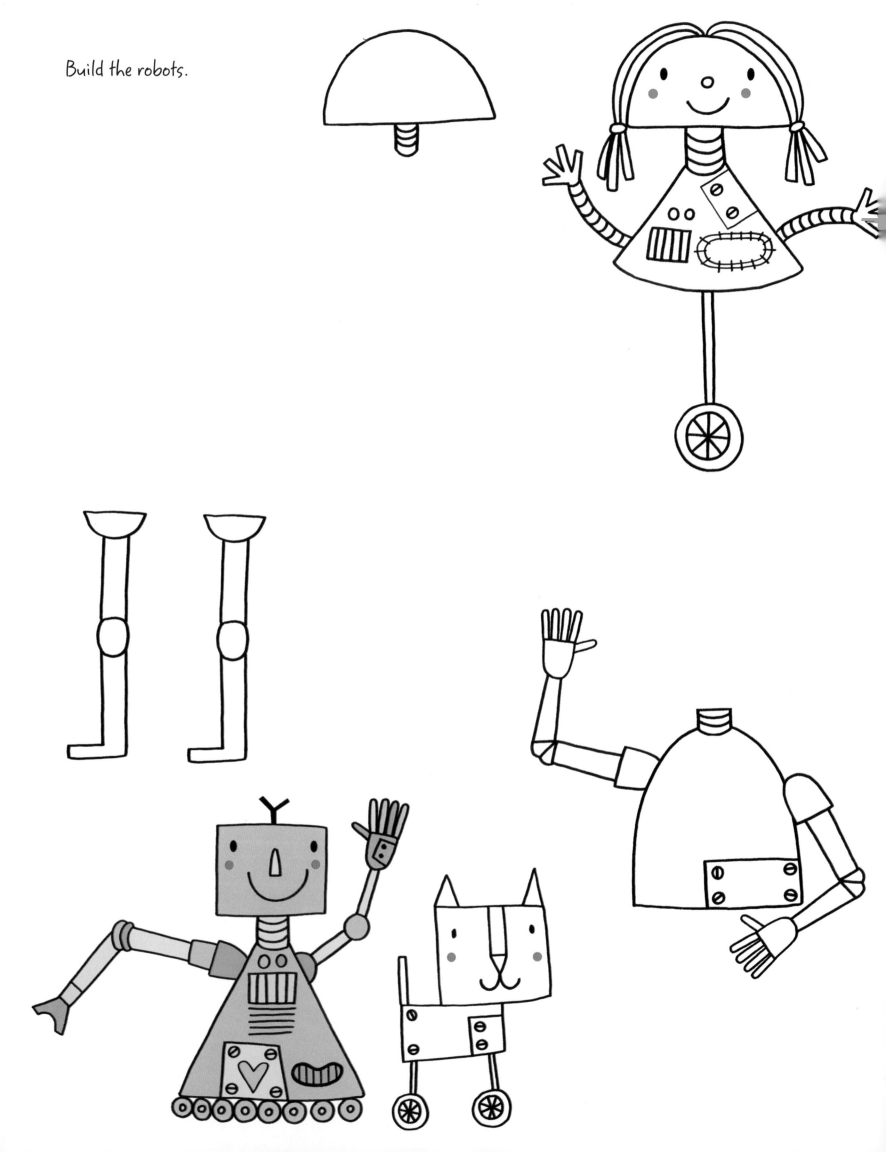

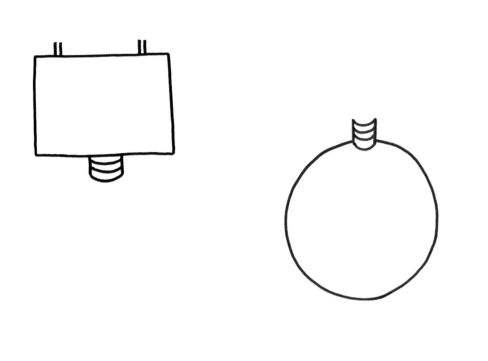

Give them buttons,
dials, lights and wheels.

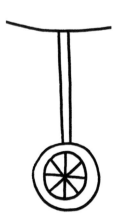

Doodle red patterns on the doves.

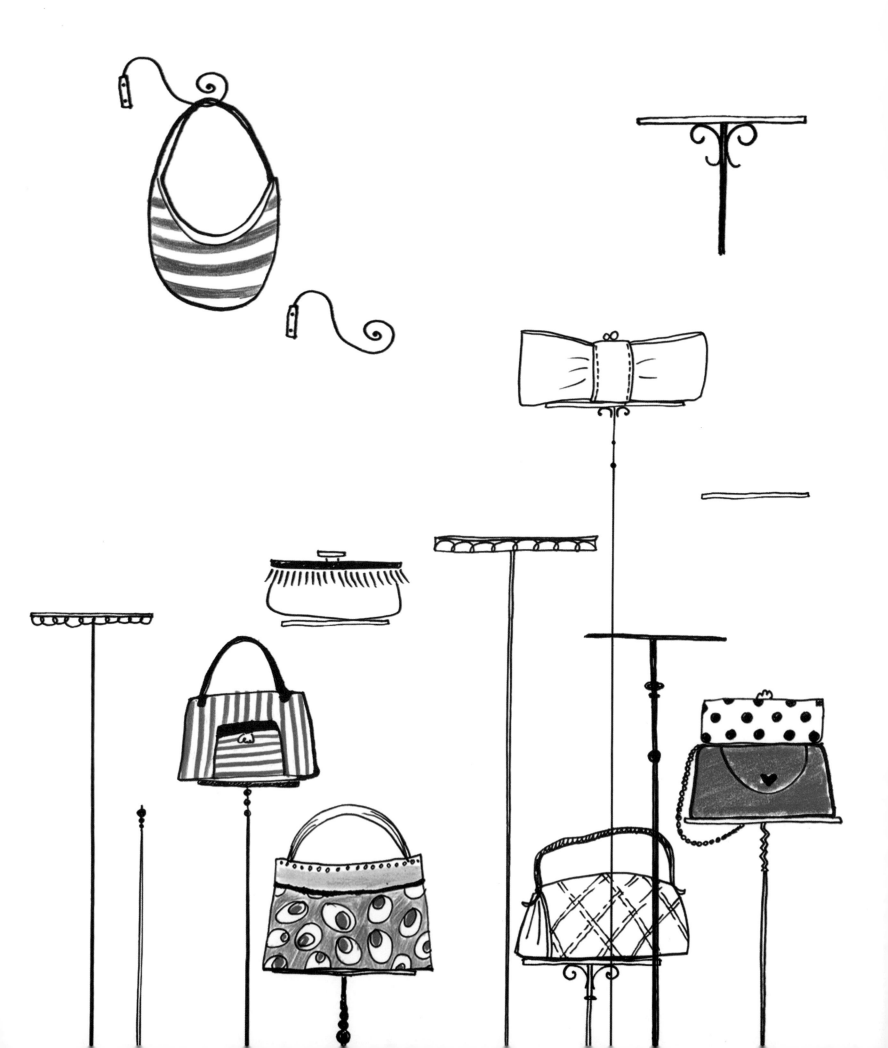

Fashionable, practical, casual or stylish?

Doodle designer bags on the stands.

Yummy red
strawberries...

Chocolate icing...

Smiling faces...

7

Doodle bright patterns on the fish.

Draw birds on the branches and leaves on the tree.

Doodle patterns to turn these shapes into snowflakes.

Doodle what you think might be stored in the jars.

Doodle more spiders and flies.

Doodle more frogs...

...and lily pads for them to jump onto.

Fill the page with zigzag patterns.

Doodle lots more bright
toadstools sprouting up.

Doodle more flowers and buzzing bees.

Party clothes, ballgowns, evening dresses, wedding dresses...

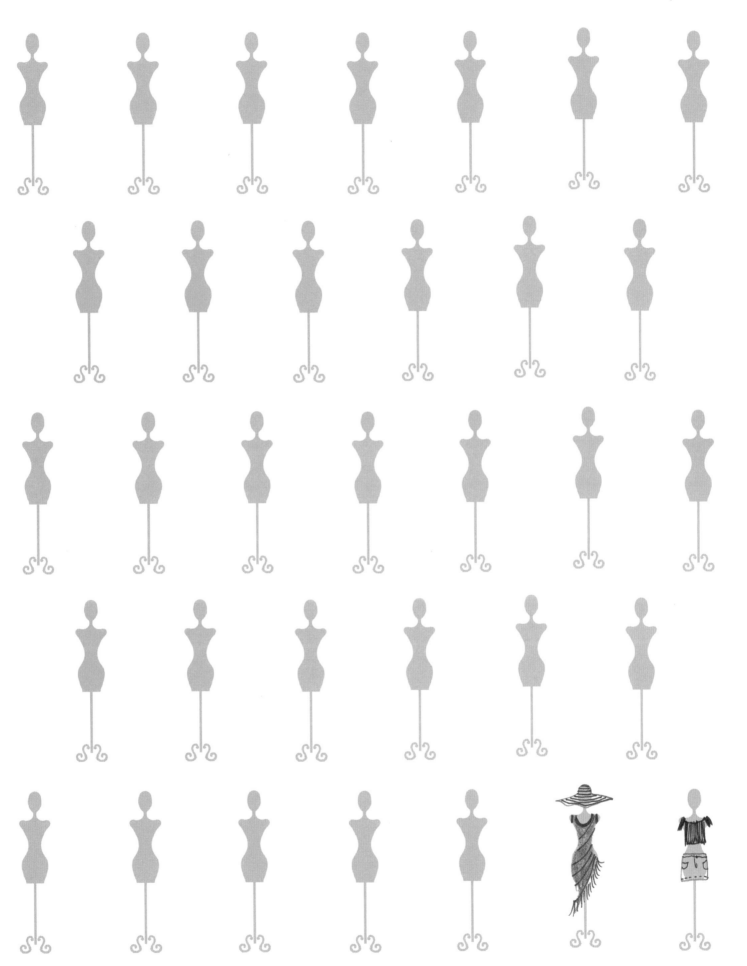

...frills, stripes, long, short?

Decorate.

Design.

Customize.

Copy the lacy patterns onto the unfinished squares or design some new ones of your own.

Doodle black fish swimming in the sea.

Add some coral and seaweed too.

Doodle cages for
the songbirds.

Draw more houses, trees, bushes and fences.

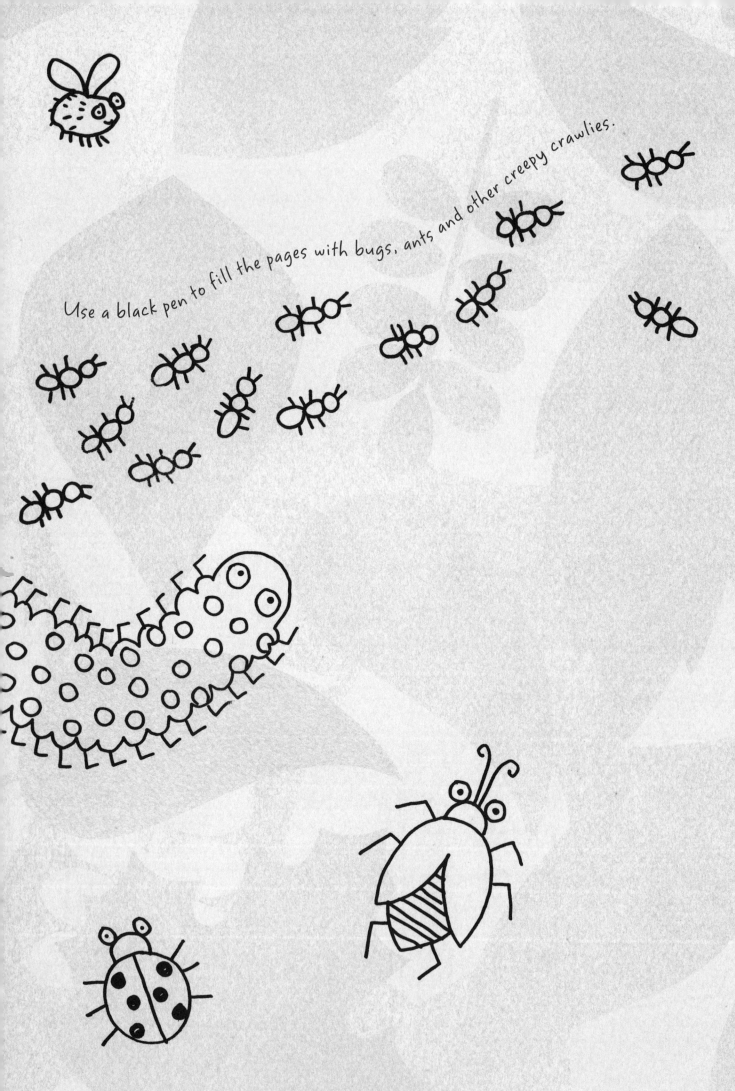

Use a black pen to fill the pages with bugs, ants and other creepy crawlies.

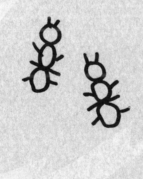

Decorate the umbrellas.

Fill the window with cupcakes, pastries and cakes.

Draw flowers in the empty vases...

...and decorate them, too.

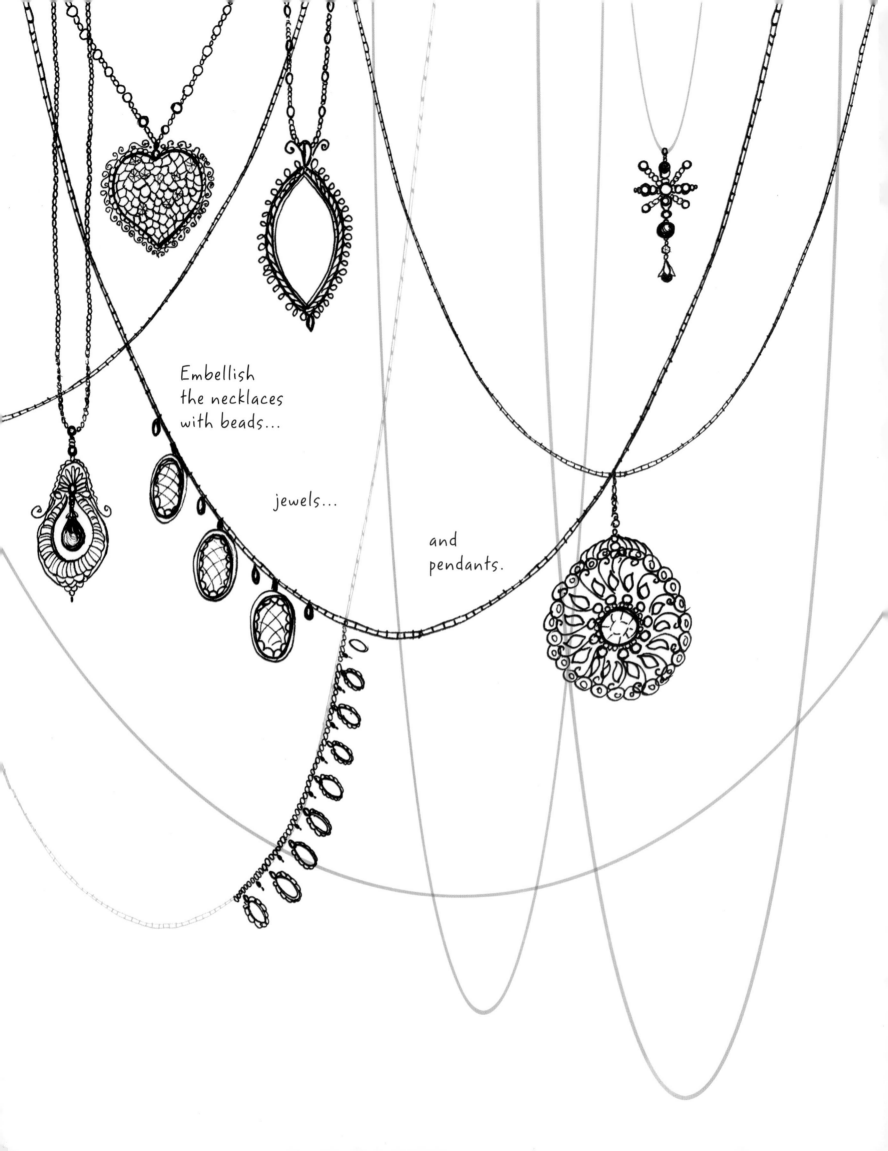

Embellish
the necklaces
with beads...

jewels...

and
pendants.